# What Happens in Camp

by

Emmylou Kotzé

PINK HYDRA PRESS

2025

Copyright

What Happens in Camp
© Emmylou Kotzé 2025

Paperback: 978-0-6398431-4-8
e-book: 978-0-6398431-5-5

Pink Hydra Press
www.thepinkhydra.com

# What Happens in Camp

# I
# Commander

"THIS WON'T HURT," his lover promised, entering him for the first time, and despite his apprehension Sage closed his eyes and allowed it to happen, bore momentary discomfort with no more than a soft gasp, a sick kind of excitement stirring deep in his guts as he admitted something into his body that was a lot thicker and more intimate than mere fingers.

Then suddenly the white-hot confusion of real pain assailed him, and he yelped loudly. "Vik!—"

"Sorry," Viktor muttered, and drew back just a half-inch or less, keeping Sage at the very threshold of discomfort as he slowed his advance.

Viktor was his best friend in all the world. They took

care of each other amidst the dirt and pain and pure chaos of war, and Sage would let him have whatever he wanted. A moment's pain didn't matter, especially not when Viktor had just given him the most exquisite pleasure of his life, swallowing down his seed as Sage writhed into the soiled sheets of his lover's bedroll.

Viktor halted, added more of the oil, carefully slicking it around the area where they were joined. It was mink tallow, which they normally used for conditioning leather. Sage could smell it, the sharp musky animal smell, and feel that the stuff was chilled solid and difficult to melt into the silky lubricant they needed. But it warmed with the heat of their bodies; Sage was almost too hot as he reclined hips upward upon the bedroll, turning his face into the stained pillow that smelled of his lover's sweat.

Viktor thrust deeper, whispering more assurances and promises, and Sage gave a sudden gasp not of pain, but of pleasurable surprise. No-one had ever told him that this might feel good for *him*; he had had no forewarning of the cresting pleasure that now welled up from deep inside, turning his cries of discomfort into hoarse moans of delight.

"I hate the thought of someone else fucking you," Viktor said quietly.

"I don't have a choice," Sage said. "*We* don't have a choice."

Viktor stood by the flap of their tent, anguish written across his broad freckled face, tall and resplendent in his cavalry uniform. He had patrol duty tonight, and a dozen underlings awaiting him, and was already late.

Next to him, Sage was diminutive and dark, half from gypsy stock (on his mother's side), and had occasionally been mistaken for a woman. He didn't mind that; it even gave him a modicum of protection sometimes. People were much less likely to interfere with them if they believed that Viktor, a fierce young sergeant of the mounted hussars, was keeping a gypsy *girl* in his tent. Sage dressed himself androgynously, wore his curly hair and his tunics just long enough so he could be taken for a peasant girl, and was not yet old enough that his facial hair would betray him at a distance.

Viktor did not respond to Sage's statement. "I'll be back late tonight," he said curtly, and began to lift the tentflap, then thought better of it. Carefully he secured the flap again, making sure that no-one could see them from outside, then crossed the few paces back towards Sage and kissed him hard on the mouth.

Viktor was not a man who showed affection readily; Sage could count on one hand the number of times he'd been kissed in the past month. And very seldom like this, with Viktor holding him close and cradling him like something precious, smoothing his hair back from his face. The embrace left him dazed, reaching blindly for his lover when at last he broke off and drew away.

Without any further words, Viktor stomped back to the tentflap and left, leaving Sage with nothing but a hard knot in his gut and the taste of yearning in his mouth.

Sage waited until evening, alone in the darkening tent, mending a worn pair of Viktor's boots just to occupy the time. Fear stalked waning courage inside his heart, as he kept recalling the anguish he had seen on his lover's face. But when he began to strain his eyes to see in the gloom, he knew he could delay no longer. The Commander had stipulated "evenfall," and was not known for being a patient man.

He muffled himself in a shawl and stepped outside. The sweltering heat of the day was passing in a sudden arrival of low rainclouds, and a few fat raindrops spattered to earth as he made his way towards Commander Anselm's tent. He waited for a while at a safe distance, until he saw the man himself, a true giant amongst even the high commanders, broad and brown-bearded and stern, appear and pass into the tent.

He sidled up as quick as he could, drew aside the flap. Anselm turned at the soft noise, and their eyes met as Sage stood within the dim lantern-light.

"You came," he said.

Sage set aside the shawl as he entered. His hands were trembling slightly. "Did I have any choice?"

Anselm moved towards him. He was a full foot taller than Sage, and something about him made Sage feel a way he never had in the presence of Viktor—that this was a man who could hurt him, maim him with his bare hands. One of those hands was near large enough to wrap around Sage's throat, and he stood stock still as the Commander towered over him, lifting his chin with just the tips of his fingers.

"You're lovely," he murmured. "Wasted on the sergeant. If the two of you were ever found out, what would you do?"

A draft of rainy air stirred the tentcloth behind Sage, and he shivered. "I suppose I would come to you," he replied in a low voice, "and beg for your help. You would not deny me." He laid a hand on the Commander's vambrace, and arched up to gaze into his eyes. "Not after this."

Anselm chuckled softly, and touched his hair. "I suppose I would not," he admitted. "You are very persuasive." His dark eyes sparkled. "Make yourself at home," he invited. "There is wine."

Sage shook his head. "You are still in your armour." Delicately he reached for one of Anselm's cuirass straps. "Let me help disrobe you."

Anselm smiled indulgently and moved into the centre

of the tent as they both began to tackle the buckles and straps of the armour he wore. Sage helped him with the shoulder-guards, his gorget and cuirass, the sabre and wheellock pistol which hung on his belt. He had often helped Viktor disarm and undress after a hard day's fighting. It was the kind of job a squire or friend would gladly do, and were it not for the tension which crackled almost palpably between himself and the older man, he would have felt perfectly comfortable. Together they stripped Anselm to his tunic, which he shrugged off whilst Sage bent to remove his boots.

There was something different about the presence of the man unarmed and half naked, something almost vulnerable yet mingled with a raw power Sage could only think of as virility. Hesitantly, he placed a hand upon Anselm's chest, drew his fingers through the thick pelt of dark brown hair. *So unlike Viktor.* Anselm breathed steadily as he explored, the barrel chest moving up and down against his questing hand. At last he took Sage's hand and firmly moved it away.

"Enough of that," he said, and his voice was hoarse.

"Undress for me. I want to see you."

Sage averted his eyes and, reluctantly, began to disrobe. Anselm's gaze was hungry as layer after layer dropped to the floor.

When at last Sage stood totally naked, trying with all his might not to cover anything he knew the Commander would want to see, it was Anselm's turn to touch. He did so with none of Sage's shyness, running his hands roughly over every inch of Sage as if he were a horse for sale. Sage had never experienced such a thorough exploration at Viktor's hands. The thought of his lover made him shiver with something that might have been fear, and might have been lust. He thought longingly of how Viktor would sometimes caress him under the privacy of a fur blanket, gently stroke his cock and run his wet mouth along Sage's neck and collarbones. Anselm did not seem inclined to use his mouth on Sage, and after he had satisfied his seeming curiosity, he stepped back and removed his trousers.

"Do you want me to wash first?" he asked, indicating the portable basin which stood beside him.

Sage shrugged, not knowing what to say. Many was the

time that Viktor had taken him after a long day's work, after a long night's drinking, at the end of a terrible battle. Sage remembered blood crusted on his lover's hands, and himself gazing mesmerized at those hands whilst Viktor was deep in the throes of his pleasure, wondering what manner of man the blood had belonged to, and precisely how he had met his end at Viktor's hands. Viktor did not ever like to talk about the battles he had been in. Sage told himself, often, that he should simply be grateful that his lover always returned to him afterwards.

In the end, Anselm washed only his crotch, gazing at Sage all the while he did so. He stroked his cock until it was fully erect, and Sage saw with a chill of apprehension that its size was perfectly in line with the rest of him.

Anselm took his hand and led him over to the bedroll in the corner. Sage went in a daze, his mouth completely dry, heart now thumping in his chest.

Anselm pulled him down to the bedroll and turned him over, arranging him with his knees apart and wide open, completely bared to his view. There was a hollow pit in the bottom of Sage's stomach, a mixture of fear and sick excitement. He closed his eyes, wondering if Anselm was going to take him completely unprepared. Viktor had never yet made him bleed, but he knew it was a possibility, and the thought made his guts roil.

But despite all his apprehension, Anselm turned out to be gentler than Viktor often was. He slicked Sage well with a specially prepared, warmed oil, no spur-of-the-moment tallow or cooking oil or even, god forbid, his own spit; and though he was handsomely endowed, he went slowly, using his fingers in the way Viktor had that first time, long ago, and sensuously sliding his erect cock up and down along Sage's ass to open him further.

By the time Anselm finally mounted him, Sage was comfortably stretched out and quivering with yearning. He cried out when Anselm began to move inside him, large hands holding his hips securely in place, and he could not tell, himself, whether it was a sound of reluctance or encouragement.

Anselm rode him with incredibly slow strokes, letting him feel the whole length that glided inexorably in and out of him. The intense pleasure that gripped Sage felt absolutely humiliating, and in a perverse way the shame of it made him even more aroused, until he had to grip his own cock or explode.

He braced himself with his hips spread wide open, Anselm fucking him rhythmically and steadily, his own cock sliding back and forth in his hand with every hard thrust. The length and girth of the man was nothing he had experienced before, and even as he whimpered with pleasure he could not say whether he truly did want this. He was impaled upon the length of that incredible spear, the pressure of it hard against the little nub of delight that Viktor had so often located inside him.

Anselm began to change his rhythm, fucking him rough and fast, and the pressure built inside Sage until it was unbearable. A series of hoarse, stuttering cries escaped him; he wept, bending his head to the pillow, and intense pleasure continued to wrack his body even after his cock had spurted long strings of stickiness all over the bedroll beneath him.

And through it all Anselm unmercifully maintained his pace, not sparing him a single moment to catch his breath. He was helpless in the man's huge hands, reduced to nothing more than a soft receptacle for his iron length. When Anselm placed one of those hands at the back of Sage's neck, he tensed, but knew there was nothing he could do.

Luckily, Anselm did not seem to wish to strangle him; the hand moved down to his shoulders, then to the small of his back, holding him more firmly in place as the Commander buried his cock inside as deep as it would go.

With Viktor, release would always be followed by a moment of intense intimacy; a tender bite on the shoulder, his hot breath against Sage's back as he panted out his relief, a trail of wet kisses down his spine or an affectionate tousle of his hair. When, after a long and gruelling ride, Anselm finally broke in his rhythm and stuttered out his spurt of ecstasy, he did none of these things. He remained inside and erect for a while, panting, his hands still gripping Sage's hips, then he unceremoniously slid out his cock and stood up, passing Sage a damp rag from the basin.

Self-consciously he cleaned himself as Anselm watched. The Commander then collapsed onto the soiled bedroll with a deep sigh of satisfaction, stretching his arm out over his head.

"That was good. Are you going to stay?"

Sage looked away. "Do you want me to?"

"No odds to me." Anselm grinned. "We'll do this again regardless."

Sage said nothing, and Anselm looked sleepily over at him.

"You enjoyed yourself."

There was no point in Sage denying it; his own body had betrayed him, laying him in spasms of pleasure whilst he was impaled upon the Commander's cock, and he knew that he had cried out loudly in ecstasy, giving Anselm the kind of sweet song he could not remember ever having given Viktor.

Anselm stretched out his arm as if awaiting him, and Sage drew into himself as he knelt on the edge of the blanket.

If he curled up here, inside Anselm's own bedroll, he knew what would happen. At some point the man would wake and want him for a second time, and Sage did not know whether he could stand such a ride again so soon, either in body or wit. The experience had disoriented him, turning the slight discomfort in his body into a hard, churning mass. He felt empty and used, and some small part of him wished perversely that the man had made him hurt and bleed, rather than giving him pleasure.

But the alternative was to return to Viktor, to meet his lover inside their shared tent after a long night of patrol duty, with his asshole fucked open, still tender with another man's seed dribbling out of him. Anselm had been sheathed deep at the moment of climax, and Sage thought he could still feel it inside him, wet and burning.

Whenever he came off patrol duty, Viktor often liked to take him for a quick, hard fuck before falling into an exhausted sleep. Tonight, he would have to contend with the Commander's semen inside there already, and know that Sage was loose and wet because of the girth of the Commander's cock, and the copious quantity of his climax.

A loud snore interrupted Sage's chain of thought, and he looked over to realize that Anselm had fallen fast asleep.

Precisely as he had feared, Sage woke with the dawn to feel the rigidity of Anselm's enormous cock pressed up against him, and the surprisingly feather-light touch of his fingers along his upper arm.

"Are you awake?" Anselm whispered in his ear.

Sage swallowed with difficulty, inclining his head. His whole body was rigid, and he gave a little gasp of pain as Anselm slid in a careful finger to investigate him.

"Still sore, then?" Anselm caressed his hip, and heaved a sigh that Sage could feel stir his hair.

Sage was silent. The first night they'd ever had sex, Viktor had taken him again the very next morning, easing him into it despite the soreness, with tender kisses along his neck and whispered words of love. The bruises had added an aching sweetness to that coupling, and Sage had found it even more pleasurable than the first time around. They seldom fucked like that, these days; not with the fighting the way it was going, and Viktor's responsibilities as he gained in rank.

Anselm released him, and settled back. "Well, I suppose I've a use for that pretty mouth of yours, then. I shouldn't think that's too sore."

"No." Anselm had not kissed him once last night, not even to set him at ease. Sage rolled over. Anselm was waiting, legs spread wide apart, his cock already erect, glistening at the tip, set tantalizingly within a bristly bush of black pubic hair.

Sage remembered his first kiss with Viktor, stolen in the darkness and secrecy of their tent, the tingle of surprise and excitement he'd felt as Viktor began to touch him, both of them still half-drunk from the night's revelry amongst the other soldiers.

"C'mon," he remembered Viktor saying, as he gently turned him over, "let me have my pleasure, the way I like it. I won't hurt you. I promise."

Sage stretched his mouth around the older man's cock, and tasted salt in the back of his throat.

# II

# Coin

THE COMMANDER LAY with his head staved in. Sage could not avert his eyes.

Yesterday, this man had been whole and virile, strong as an ox, and had ruthlessly dominated all other men. Today, he lay helpless, brought low by a young hussar who did not even possess a full beard.

He lay with Viktor in the afterdawn light that penetrated their tent. Sage could not look at him. With every breath he took, he could feel where the Commander's cock had been.

"How many times?" Viktor asked in a low voice.

"Just once."

"Only once?"

Sage swallowed. He still had the salt-bitter taste of the man's semen in his mouth. "Twice."

Viktor looked askance at him.

"Once in the ass, once in the mouth," Sage clarified, shamefacedly.

Viktor grunted. "Just as well you warned me," he said, and his voice was low and dangerous. "I was going to kiss you."

He suddenly got to his knees and seized Sage, roughly turning him over onto his stomach. Sage let out a surprised cry as Viktor straddled him from behind, pulling his under-breeches down until they caught between his knees. Viktor spat into his hand. Sage's heart raced; his head spun. Viktor began to rub his hand up and down along Sage's already tender asshole, and he panted in confusion, wanting to ask Viktor to stop yet not having the heart to.

Without any more warning or preparation, Viktor thrust his hard cock into Sage and began to fuck him. There was some pleasure there, but it was lost amongst discomfort and the deep shame Sage felt and the violence with which Viktor assaulted him. It went on and on; Sage could hear himself keening like a wounded animal, and the grunts of effort Viktor made as he pounded away.

He remembered how once Viktor had come into their tent after a fight amongst the younger hussars, pale under his freckles, blood up to his elbows, something that looked like dried bits of kidney crusted to his hands. Sage had helped wash it off, whatever it had been. Once the image and the comparison sprang into his mind, it would not leave him.

After that, it became almost a ritual. Sage would visit Anselm every few days, whenever the summons came, and every time the Commander would remind him of what might happen should he refuse. *If they knew that their stalwart young sergeant was keeping a boy in his tent.*

Anselm would fuck him wide open until Sage was loose and dripping, and then he would return in shame to Viktor, who would take his turn with a brutality that Sage had never thought would be directed at *him*. He would be miserable afterwards, bruised and sore, sobbing in Viktor's embrace. Sometimes Viktor would apologize, kiss and hold him, tuck him gently into his arms as he drifted off to sleep. Other times, he would push Sage roughly away from him, get up and dress and leave the tent, leaving him in a quivering heap beneath the blankets. Sage had no idea where Viktor went on those nights, and the abandonment seemed far worse than the pain, which never lasted more than a day or two.

In death, the man's ruined face seemed almost noble, fair and ruddy, and Sage wondered what it might have been like to kiss those lips, not nearly as cold now as they had been in life. Their last two encounters haunted him.

The inexorable summons came, and Sage obeyed with a hard knot of anxiety in his stomach. Viktor had had him roughly just the previous night, and he knew that something was wrong.

Anselm got him down in his preferred position, on all fours, and as usual began to prepare him with his fingers.

Sage yelped loudly in pain; Anselm withdrew immediately, a sharp intake of breath betraying his shock. There was blood on his fingers, which Sage could just see from his current vantage, peering over his own shoulder.

Wordlessly Anselm stood up and cleansed his hand, then returned to Sage, used his mouth instead, let him return to Viktor within an hour with obvious reluctance.

Viktor received him with nothing but a scowl. "You're back early."

Haltingly, trembling with shame, Sage told Viktor what had happened. He would never forget the look on his face afterwards.

For ten days, Sage did not hear from the Commander. He did not hear much from Viktor either. He mostly lay in bed, recovering. Viktor made sure he had all he needed, food and wine and even some rather dubious ointment he claimed had been prepared by the camp surgeon. He did not touch Sage, not even to hold his hand or caress his brow, and every night he went out. He would return just before dawn, stinking of cheap beer and something else, a scent Sage found unfamiliar yet suggestive, and he would crawl into bed beside Sage and fall asleep immediately upon his return.

Just as Sage began to wonder whether perhaps Anselm had lost interest in him, the message arrived, summoning him for the night.

He left secretly, without telling Viktor, who had once again disappeared without a word. Anselm received him eagerly, readied him quickly, and they fucked on the Turkish mat with Sage leaning back on his knees, hand gripped tightly around his own cock as Anselm thrust into him. He was past pretending, now, that he did not relish these encounters. Anselm took a lot longer than Viktor usually did, starting out slow and deep, giving Sage all the time he needed to bring himself to climax.

Anselm's breath hitched behind Sage, his cock twitching in unmistakable release. There was the usual easing of pressure as Anselm slid out of him. He remained on his knees, knowing that the Commander often liked to survey his own handiwork afterwards.

Anselm breathed a deep sigh, stirring Sage's hair. Carefully, he laid his head against Sage's shoulder.

Sage stiffened in what was almost fright. This was as close as Anselm had ever come to kissing him.

"You don't have to go back," the Commander murmured into his ear.

"And what would I do instead?" Sage's heart pounded in his chest.

"You can stay here," Anselm responded. "You're wasted on the sergeant. One day, he's going to beat you to death. How badly will he hurt you, when you return?"

Sage felt like crying, and a sudden, helpless anger knotted inside his gut. He did not respond.

"Think about it," Anselm said, getting to his feet and handing Sage the customary rag. "I would hate to see that lovely face of yours beneath a shroud."

Blind anger glittered in Viktor's pale eyes. "You went to him?"

Sage breathed out, slowly. "I did."

"And he fucked you?" Viktor demanded. "You're recovered?"

Sage nodded, and began to undress, pulling off his tunic quickly, then slipping down his breeches.

Viktor stared at him. "What the fuck are you doing?"

"You're going to take me, I know," Sage gave back. "Just—Vik, just please make it as gentle as you can." He turned himself around and got onto all fours. Cold air kissed the wetness around his asshole. He heard Viktor move, and closed his eyes in dread anticipation.

Nothing happened. No-one touched him. There was silence in the tent. Sage looked over his shoulder. Viktor had gone.

Now he looked down at the face of the dead man, and guilt and fear and self-loathing roiled in his gut.

The Commander's murder was a complete mystery, and Sage had heard several dozen unlikely stories on his way here. They had found him like this, in his tent at dawn, head staved in with the murder weapon abandoned beside him. A peasant's club, riven with rusted nails.

Sage had always known that Viktor was a violent man. He had always been aware that the man he called lover had killed other men, in many brutal ways.

Sage had never, and would never, kill anyone. He would rather be violated himself than ever risk hurting another. He had never chosen war; the war had come to him, rolling inexorably across the fields and farms of central Europe, and he had simply been caught up in it. He had come of age in war, and the man he loved above all others was an instrument of war, a weapon full as deadly as the cavalryman's sabre or the matchlock rifle.

He bowed his head one last time. It would not do to linger for too long. The soldier standing vigil over Anselm's body took no notice as he scuttled away.

"I'm going out," Viktor announced at dusk. Sage was mending a shirt, and the needle slipped in his hand, stabbing a finger. Blood welled up, staining the plain white cloth. Sage looked up, saw Viktor ready to leave already, standing at the tentflap.

"Where to?" he asked hollowly.

"Drinking."

Sage blinked. Viktor had not so much as touched him since that day he bled. Not to kiss, not to caress, not to love.

Blood soaked into the garment he was holding.

"You murdered him," he whispered, and Viktor looked back, startled. "What's going to become of us?"

"Nothing will happen," Viktor returned, "so long as no-one finds out. And who's going to tell them? You?"

"Perhaps." Sage's voice was audible, though tiny, and Viktor looked thunderstruck.

"I have killed men for far less than what he did," he returned at last. "Don't you try me, Sage. Not *you*."

He turned and was gone before Sage could respond, and Sage choked on the things left unsaid.

The moon rose as Sage waited for Viktor to return, biting his fingernails in his anxiety, dark thoughts churning inside him. He thought of what he would say to Viktor when he returned. His planned speech grew angrier and angrier as the hours passed by, until he pictured himself seizing the rifle which leaned against Viktor's gear in the corner, using it to beat Viktor, to punish him, to make him bleed.

At last Sage could take it no longer. It was past midnight, but sleep would not come for him, not tonight. He left their tent and made a circuit of the camp, of Viktor's favourite drinking-places. He was nowhere to be found. No-one appeared even to have seen him.

Desperation and anxiety lay leaden in Sage's heart, and he stumbled as he navigated through the shadows. This was the part of camp where men went for entertainment and diversions, and it was past drinking-time. The noises of a woman in the throes of passion drifted somewhere on the wind, and the flickering fires in the pits burned low.

"Whoa there, pretty bit." A big man suddenly loomed up before Sage, seizing his arm. "How much for the night?"

Sage glanced up in sudden fear, nervously smoothed the thin hairs on his lip that should be obvious at this vantage, even in the dark. "I'm not a woman," he stammered.

The man snorted. "I can see that." He grabbed Sage's other wrist, pinning him in place. "*How much?*"

Sage froze in panic. It was not the first time something like this had happened, but in the past, Viktor had never been more than a few yards away. Usually the sight of the tall young hussar, with his attendant scowl, was more than enough to discourage even the most determined whoremonger, and Vik was not in the least bit shy to use his fists on those few who weren't.

But tonight, Sage had no idea where Viktor even was, and the man accosting him was nowhere near drunk enough for him to slip away. He was young, as tall as Viktor but broader, with eyes hard as flints and bushy yellow mustachios set over a brutal mouth.

Unable to think of anything else to do, Sage named a sum.

The man released him, and nodded curtly. "To my tent, then. Come."

Sage allowed the man to take his arm, as his emotions warred within him. He wanted to pull free and run. He wanted Viktor. But what did it even matter? Whatever bond had existed between the two of them, it was irreparably broken now.

As a camp follower, before he met Viktor, Sage had mended boots, polished knives, melted scrap lead into balls to sell as extra shot to soldiers. The idea of selling his body had never occurred to him.

He came back to himself with a start, naked with a stranger in a strange tent, being embraced and touched by a man whose name he did not know. He was kissed roughly, pushed down onto a camp cot, his legs manoeuvred apart and up. His own shyness and reluctance only seemed to inflame the man's passions. He was penetrated hard and fast, the sticky oil the stranger had fished out from some crevice of his belongings quite inadequate to the task. He made an effort not to cry out in pain, but he wasn't sure it even mattered. The man made him stay the night, had him twice again before morning, and paid him with a handful of silver coins.

Before full dawn, Sage returned to the silent tent where they had lived together for so long. Viktor was nowhere to be seen. Sage gathered his meagre possessions and left. He thought of leaving a note, but there was no paper. He thought of leaving a message with their neighbour, but could not think of what to say. By evening, he had used some of his silver to install himself in a tent of his own among the camp followers, and was being fucked vigorously up the ass by yet another stranger. At least this time, he had had the foresight to get himself the right kind of oil.

It took Viktor the better part of a week to find him.

It was late, Sage had just entertained what he hoped would be his last patron for the night, and he was cleaning himself with trembling hands when the tentflap lifted without warning. He turned angrily, only to find himself face-to-face with the man he had called lover for so long.

Sage braced himself, noticing that he carried no weapon, yet he felt certain that Viktor was capable of killing someone with his bare hands. For half a heartbeat they stared at each other; Sage shook his loose bedgown down around his thighs, and Viktor's breath hitched in his throat.

Viktor crossed the room, and scooped Sage into his arms.

Taken quite aback, Sage could only stand there while

Viktor embraced him, held him fast. Viktor's face was flushed; he made as if to kiss Sage, but Sage turned his face away.

"What do you think you're playing at?" Viktor's voice was rough.

"Release me," Sage whispered. "I'm not yours any more."

Viktor stood back, gazing intently at him. Sage averted his eyes. He drew his gown more tightly about himself, hiding the arousal that had just risen up white-hot and unexpected inside him.

"If you're here to fuck me, Viktor, you'll have to pay me," he said. "Like anyone else."

"I'm not here to fuck you," Viktor returned.

"Then leave."

Viktor glared at him; Sage met his gaze unflinchingly. He was not afraid of Viktor; he never had been. If he were to die by another man's hand, better it should be one who loved him, who would weep inconsolably even as his hard fingers tightened around his throat. To die like Anselm, beaten like a dog and cast aside by his enemy, would be intolerable.

"I swore once, Sage," Viktor said hoarsely, "that I'd kill anyone who dared even touch you."

He could not hold back a bitter laugh. "You'd have to kill half the camp by now, Vik."

True pain flashed across Viktor's face, so fast that Sage could have missed it by blinking. "Tell me why, Sage," he said softly.

"If you don't already know," Sage whispered, "then I have nothing to say to you." His hands trembled, and he clenched them on the hem of his gown. "If you've nothing to do here," he continued, "then go. I'm tired. I need to sleep."

"Fine." Viktor flashed a silver coin at him, and Sage reached out unconsciously to take it. "Does this buy me some time with you?"

Sage hesitated. "Viktor . . ." He looked quickly up into the young hussar's face, noting his carefully controlled expression, the way Viktor seemed to be holding something inside in check with all his might. "How about this," he heard himself say. "I don't need the silver. Take back your coin, and you can do whatever you want to me, if you answer just one question."

"Tell me the question," Viktor growled.

"Those nights the past few weeks, when you left me alone in our tent," Sage said, and saw Viktor flinch. "Where did you go?"

Viktor reached out and took the coin from him. For a moment it seemed as if he might simply leave, and abandon Sage once more. But then he replied, hoarsely: "Different places. Usually, drinking. But if it was too late—"

"To fuck someone else," Sage supplied, and Viktor did not deny it. "Whores?"

"Only women," Viktor said softly. "As I'm sure *you* know, Sage, it's harder to find men who are willing."

"As if it makes any difference," Sage returned bitterly.

Viktor shrugged. There seemed no more to say. Sage remembered what he had promised Viktor in return for his honesty, and his guts twisted even as warmth rose through him.

At last he took Viktor's unresisting hand, and led him through a tattered curtain to the back of the tent where he slept and fucked upon a straw mattress that smelled to him of all the men who had been here already.

He slipped off the bedgown, then reached for Viktor, who seemed oddly hesitant. It had always been him pulling the clothes off Sage, not the other way around. But Sage would be damned if it was said of him that he hadn't kept a bargain, and slowly he undressed Viktor, shirt and shoes and belt, sliding his trousers down to find that he was full as aroused as Sage was. He began to touch Viktor: the hard ridges of his bony hands and wrists, the freckled chest as smooth and white as cream, the peach-fuzz on his face.

Suddenly, Viktor drew him close and kissed him, hard and deep, and pushed him down to the mattress. The fiery desire that rose up between the two of them burned all else away, and Sage keened in delight as Viktor continued to kiss him, laid him on his back with his legs apart, and climbed atop him, continuing his gentle caresses. Sage waited, quivering in anticipation, but something was wrong. He felt Viktor's cock probe gently at him, then withdraw.

"What's the matter?" he whispered, frustrated. "Are you—incapable?"

Viktor clenched his right hand into a fist, next to Sage's head, and he braced himself. He had never been so certain that Viktor would strike him. But the look in the hard pale eyes slowly subsided, and the fist relaxed, and Viktor stayed where he was atop Sage.

"You keep making jokes like that, in this way of work you've chosen, and you might not live very long," he said in a low, warning voice. He looked down at Sage. "How long have I got? How much time did my honesty pay for?"

Sage looked up at him, into eyes mist-pale and incomprehensible, and shook his head. "Vik—all night, if you want." His voice was thick. "What's left of the night, anyway."

"You sure? You'd have me stay all night?"

Sage's throat was dry. "For old times' sake."

Viktor nodded and rolled off him, reached for the thin blanket that lay at the foot of the mattress, spread it over them both. He turned to Sage and held him as they drifted to sleep.

Sage woke in the morning in Viktor's arms, dissatisfaction roiling inside him, the musty smell of the straw mattress irritating his nose. Viktor stirred beside him, sat up, rubbed his eyes.

"I'd best be going," he said in a low voice, and Sage bit his lip, feeling as if he were about to burst into tears.

Viktor stood up and reached for the clothes he had left on the floor, and something broke inside Sage at last.

He got to his feet, sent the clothes flying as he shoved Viktor back down to the mattress with all his might. Viktor was far too surprised to protest, and Sage straddled him, kissed him hard, touched him roughly, then leant down and put his mouth around his cock.

There was a strangled gasp of confusion from Viktor, then soft moans of pleasure as he swelled and hardened inside Sage's mouth. Sage had never done this to Viktor before, though in the past Viktor had often pleasured him this way. He had never shown any desire to have Sage reciprocate him in kind, preferring the sacred act of penetration.

Sage hung on until there could be no doubt of Viktor's capability, until he was hard, too big to fit in Sage's mouth, wet with clear slick. He lay gasping in arousal, one of his hands gripping Sage's hair almost as if to hold him off.

Sage surfaced to behold Viktor dishevelled and flushed in the face, looking up at him with a hunger only matched by Sage's own desire.

"Vik," he gasped, "I want you to fuck me. Now. I want you inside me." It was all a mess, limbs going everywhere as he drew Viktor atop himself and tried to oil his own asshole at the same time, but Viktor seemed to catch on at last. He took the oil from Sage, slicked his cock forcefully until it was dripping from the end, spread Sage's legs apart and entered him without hesitation. Pleasure spiked immediately inside Sage's body, almost too hot and overwhelming to bear. He writhed and wrapped his legs around Viktor's waist, spreading himself open for Viktor to take, and at last, he responded exactly the way Sage wanted him to.

Viktor took his hand, pressed it into the mattress as he fucked Sage with quick, hard strokes, making him yelp in breathless delight. He buried his face in Sage's neck, leaving a wide wet patch with his hot mouth. Sage gave himself over to the encounter, yielded to Viktor's dominion of his body. There was a rightness to this, a sense of wanting he had not felt when any other man gave him pleasure. It allowed him to calm down, for what felt like the first time in weeks. The Commander was no more; Viktor had taken care of that, and Sage need no longer be haunted by the ghost which stood between himself and his lover.

He reached for Viktor and drew him into a deep kiss as they coupled, clung to him, aware of every movement he made and the incredible, aching pleasure that radiated from his cock into every inch of Sage's body. Sage did not need to touch himself to reach climax; not when Viktor was this close, not when he could see in Viktor's eyes how much he wanted him, how he delighted in the secret pleasures of Sage's body.

Viktor shuddered atop him with a long, low cry, shedding his seed like a tree shaking off the last leaves of autumn, and they both lay replete, exhausted, breathing hard. Viktor's eyes, when he pulled out of Sage, were shadowed with confusion, and he seated himself cross-legged on the edge of the mattress as Sage sat up with a soft groan, pushing the filthy bedsheet away from himself.

There was a long silence, and then Viktor turned his head and spoke. "I suppose I owe you that coin after all."

Sage rolled his eyes in exasperation. "You owe me no coin," he said at last, reaching for Viktor's hand. "Take me back to our tent, Vik. When we're there, I want you to have a wash, and wash me, and then fuck me again, on our own bedroll. I don't want to smell anything but your sweat, your seed."

"Fuck, Sage," Viktor muttered. He entwined his fingers with Sage's and pulled him forcibly closer, then put a hand in his hair, holding him in place. "If you come back," he whispered hoarsely, "you'll not leave again."

"Never," Sage agreed, "but that goes for you, too." He curled himself into Viktor's chest. "If anyone so much as touches me again, I want you to kill them."

Viktor gave him a crooked grin, pulled him closer by the hair, kissed him hungrily. The camp was quiescent around them. Tomorrow, war would resume; that much was inevitable. But for today, there was a brief interlude of peace.

# Other books by Emmylou Kotzé

Amphipolitan: a poetry collection

The Broken Knight

Forest of the Morning


Short stories:

"No Deal" at White Cat Publications

"What Makes a Man" in Fall Into Fantasy by Cloaked Press


. . . and even more short stories and poetry free to read at www.amphipolitan.com!

# About Pink Hydra Press

Founded in 2024 to make a space for new, queer, and weird speculative literature, Pink Hydra Press is the only organization of its kind in Africa. The genre/lit magazine The Pink Hydra has published short stories and poems from dozens of international authors. The book press is just starting out.

If you enjoy stories with a touch of the weird, or if you're an author who loves writing books and poetry infused with weirdness, come visit us at www.thepinkhydra.com.

We publish a variety of genres, but we are particularly interested in queer science fiction and fantasy, stories written by and about women, stories which challenge the current status quo, and spicy romantic and erotic stories.

**Many heads. One mission.**

9 780639 843148